BUSH BASH!

Sally Morgan & Ambelin Kwaymullina

LITTLE HARE
www.littleharebooks.com

"One dashing dingo!
Where is he going?"
said two nosy numbats.

1
2

"One dashing dingo!
Where is he going?"
said **three** flying frogs.

3

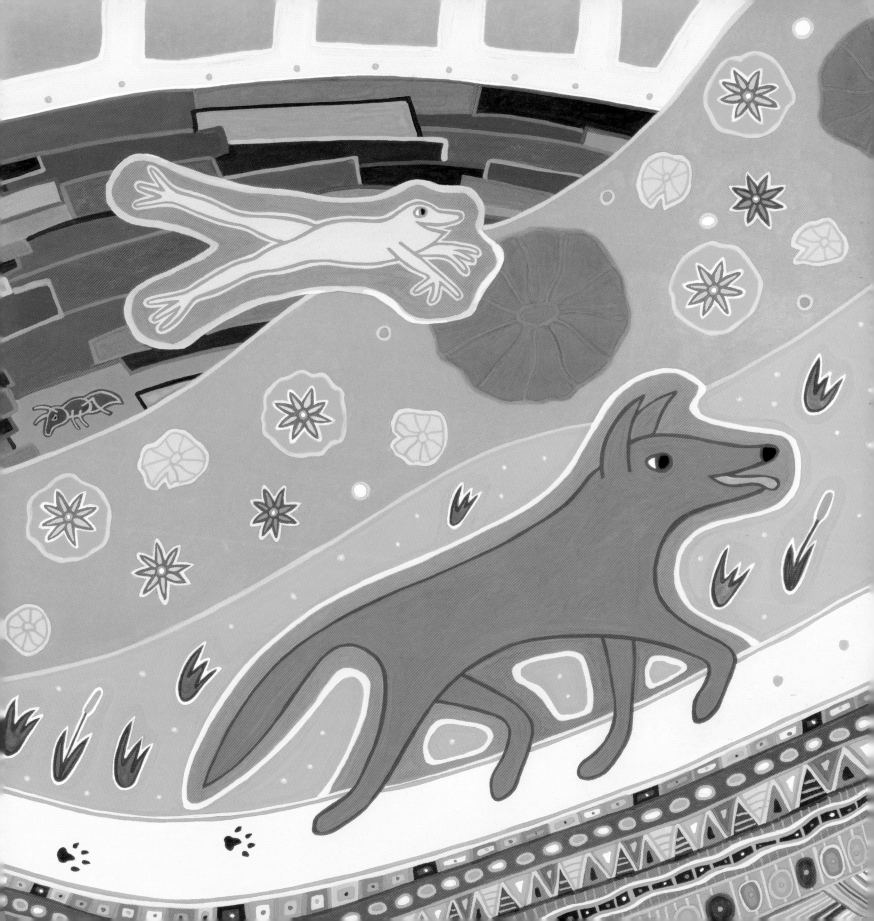

4

"One dashing dingo!
Where is he going?"
said **four** burrowing bilbies.

"One dashing dingo!
Where is he going?"
said **five** cackling crows.

5

"One dashing dingo!
Where is he going?"
said **six** waddling wombats.

6

"One dashing dingo!
Where is he going?"
said **seven** gleeful gliders.

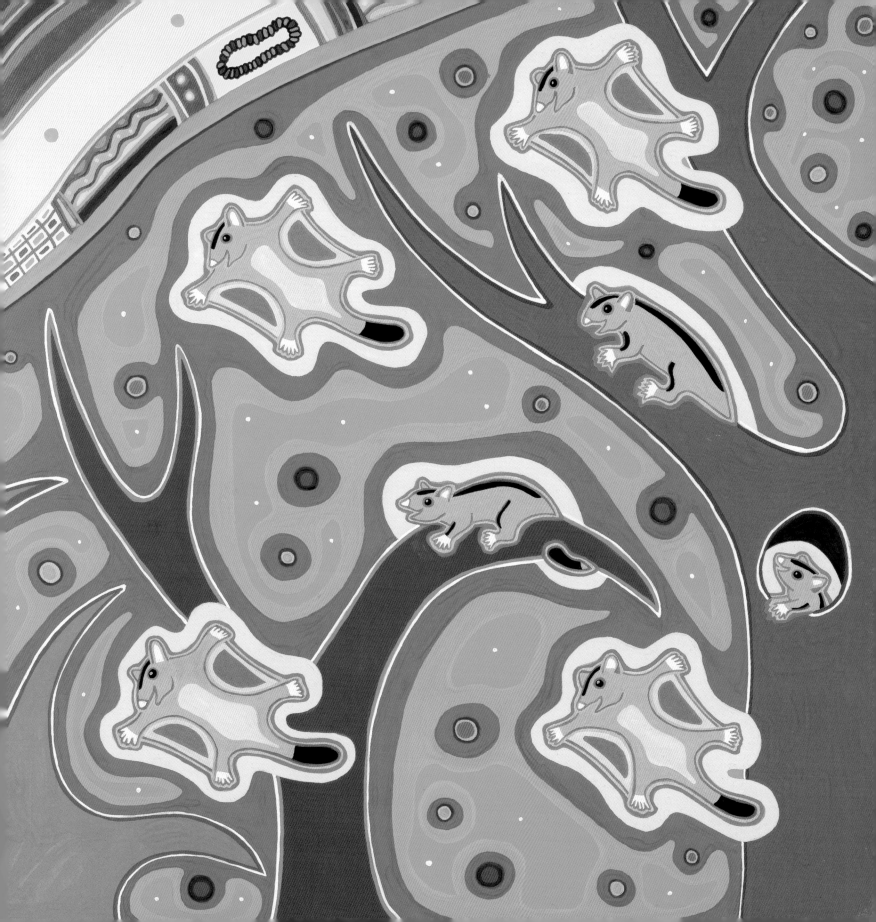

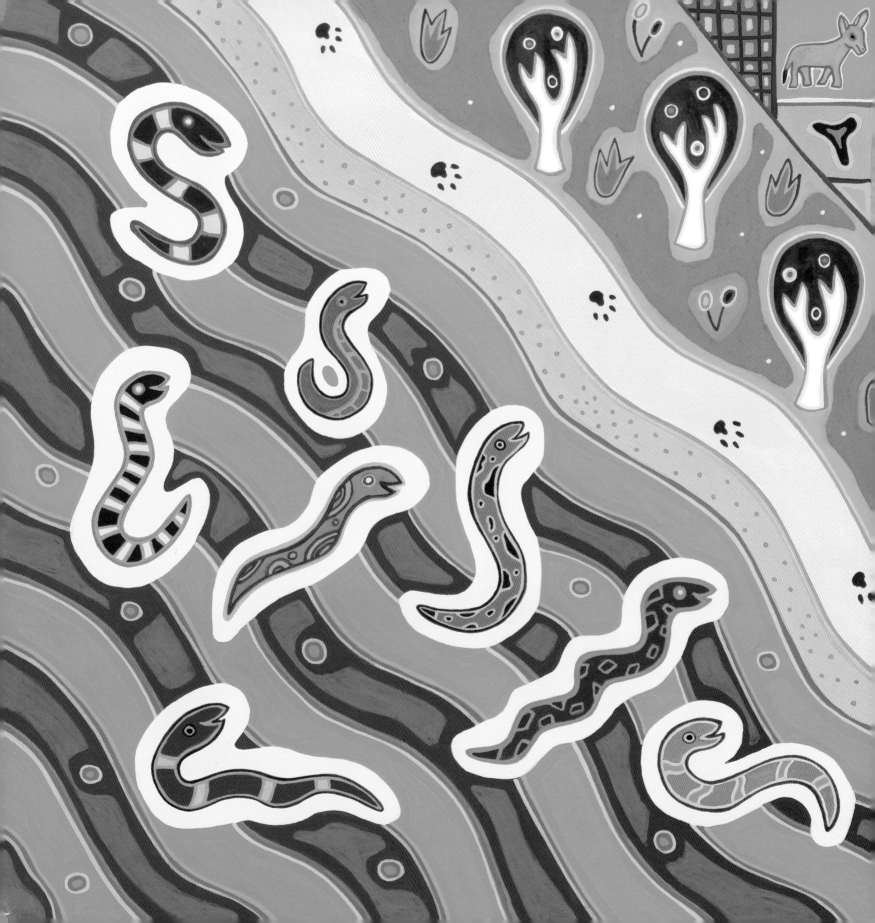

"One dashing dingo!
Where is he going?"
said **eight** slithering sea snakes.

8

"One dashing dingo!
Where is he going?"
said **nine** merry magpies.

9

10

"One dashing dingo!
Where is he going?"
said **ten** leaping lizards.

"If you follow me, you'll see,"
said Dingo.

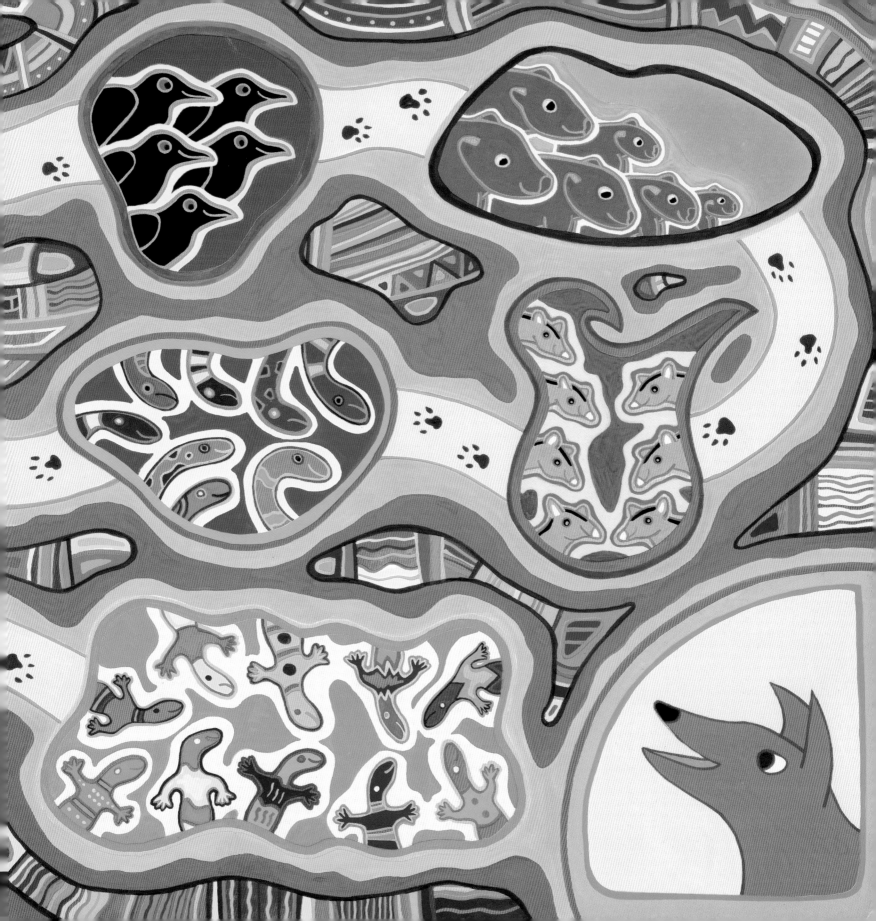

"Happy birthday, Emu!"

Hide and Seek

Here are ten pairs of objects. One of each pair is an Aboriginal object and the other is an animal that doesn't belong in the Australian bush. Can you find them all?

cane toad — dilly bag

fire ant — fish trap

feral camel — tapping sticks

feral water buffalo — spear

rabbit — didgeridoo

feral pig — seed necklace

feral donkey — carved animal

feral goat — boomerang

fox — coolamon

cat — woven basket

Here are five objects for you to find at Emu's party.

For Tiger—SM

For Paulina, who loves all our stories—AK

Little Hare Books, an imprint of Hardie Grant Egmont
Ground Floor, Building 1, 658 Church Street, Richmond, VIC 3121, Australia

www.littleharebooks.com

Text copyright © Sally Morgan 2012. Illustrations copyright © Ambelin Kwaymullina 2012

First published 2012
First published in paperback 2012 (twice)
Reprinted 2013, 2014, 2016 (twice), 2018

 A catalogue record for this book is available from the National Library of Australia

NATIONAL LIBRARY OF AUSTRALIA

ISBN 978 1 921894 14 5 (pbk.)

Designed by Xou Creative (www.xou.com.au). Produced by Pica Digital, Singapore
Printed through Asia Pacific Offset. Printed in Shenzhen, Guangdong Province, China

11 10 9 8 7